BY

ANDY GRIFFITHS

ILLUSTRATED BY TERRY DENTON

SQUARE
FISH

FEIWEL AND FRIENDS
NEW YORK, NY

SQUARE FISH

An Imprint of Macmillan

Library of Congress Control Number: 2010279103

ISBN 978-0-312-65301-9

Originally published in hardcover by Pan Macmillan Australia Pty Limited
First published in hardcover in the United States by Feiwel and Friends
Book design by Liz Seymour and Terry Denton
Square Fish logo designed by Filomena Tuosto
First Square Fish Edition: August 2010
mackids.com

10 9 8 7 6

AR: 2.2 / F&P: M / LEXILE: 380L

CONTENTS

BIG FAT COWS

It's raining
big fat cows
today.

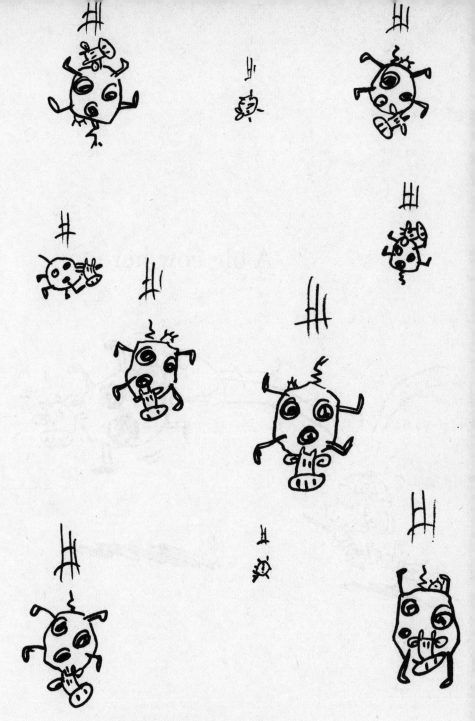

How many cows?
It's hard to say.

A big cow here.

A fat cow there.

Big fat cows are

EVERY

WHERE!

Cows underwater.

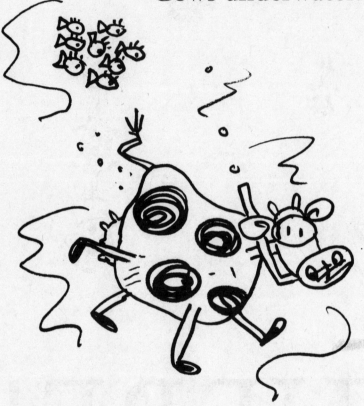

Cows in space.

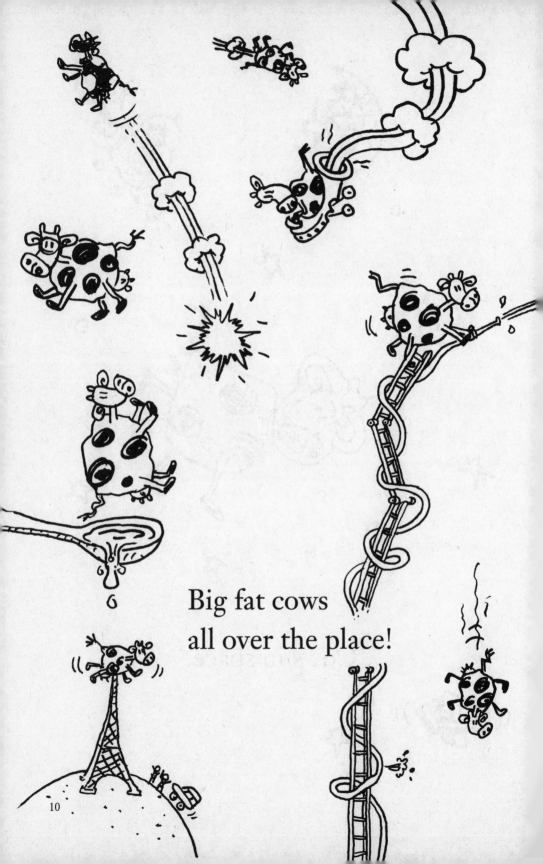

Big fat cows
all over the place!

Cows in boats.

Cows in suits.

Big fat cows
in cowboy boots!

This one is a
mixed-up cow.
It flaps its wings
and says meow!

Oh, no—watch out!

Don't look now!

This one is an

EXPLODING cow. . . .

NOEL THE MOLE

Here is a hole.

A deep,
dark
hole.

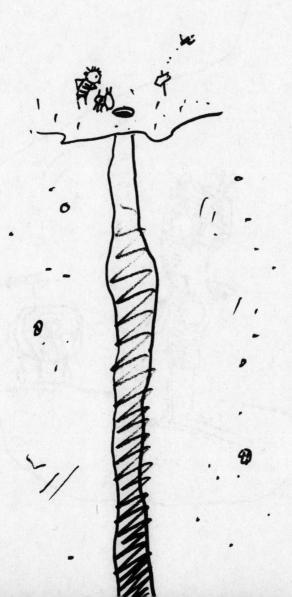

In this hole
lives a mole
called Noel.

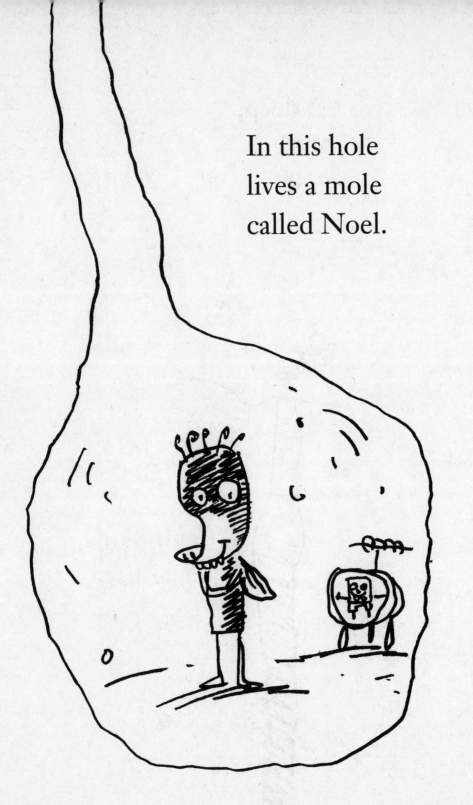

He eats
black coal.

He plays
rock and roll.

And
that's
the
whole
story
of
the
mole
called
Noel—
he's a
hole-dwelling,
coal-eating,
rock-and-roll
mole!

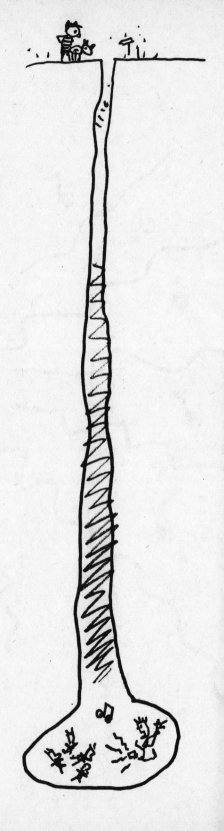

KLAUS THE MOUSE

This
is
Klaus.

Klaus
is a
mouse.

Klaus
the
mouse
has
a
very
small
house.

A

very,

very,

very,

very,

very

small
house.

But Klaus
the mouse
hates his
small house . . .

because
Klaus
is
a

VERY,

VERY,

VERY

BI

mouse!

WILLY THE WORM

This is Willy.
Willy the worm.

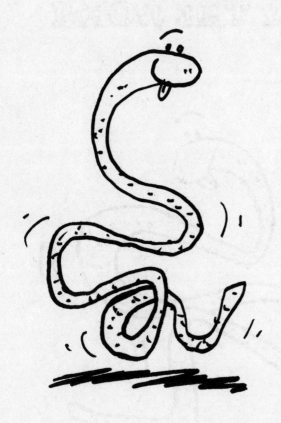

He goes to
squirm school
to learn how
to squirm.

But Willy the worm
is a very bad learner.

He's wiggly
on the
straight,

and a
terrible
turner!

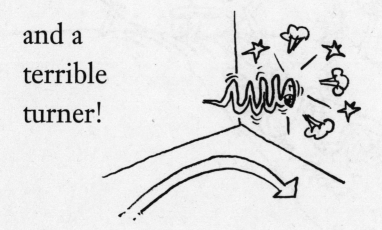

Willy never pays attention,
and he fools around a lot.

He always ends up
in a great, big knot!

KEITH, ED, AND DAISY

Here is a man
called Three-coat Keith.
He wears one coat on top
and two underneath.

Keith has a brother
called Five-hat Ed.

He wears five hats
on top of his head.

And this
is their sister,
One-dress Daisy.

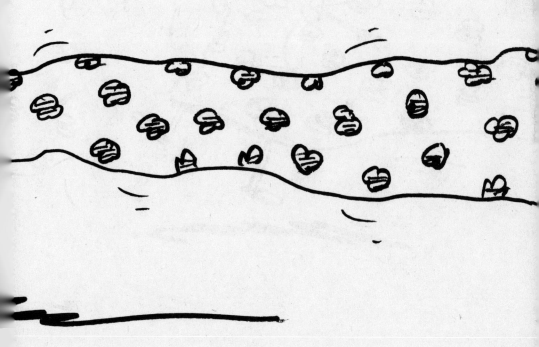

She shares her dress
with her best friend, Maisie.

LUMPY-HEAD
FRED

Have you heard
about the boy called
Lumpy-head Fred?

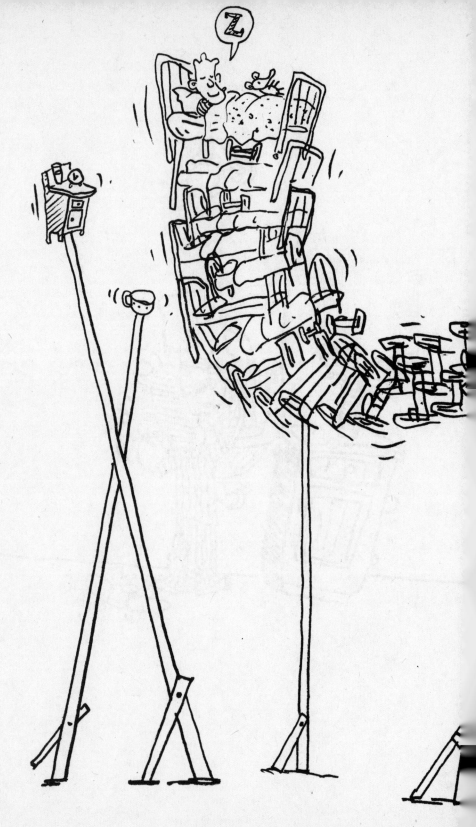

He sleeps
at the top
of a
100-decker
bed!

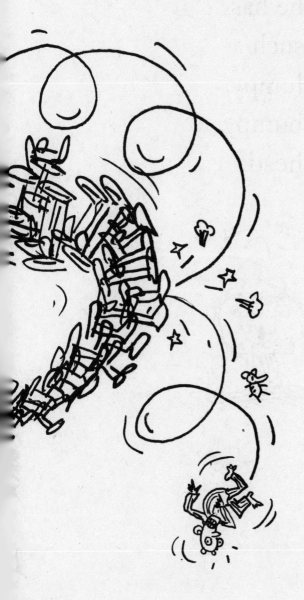

But
poor,
old
Fred
always
falls
out of
bed.

Which
is why
he has
such a
lumpy,
bumpy
head.

BRAVE DAVE

This is Dave
who, during the day,
is

REALLY,

REALLY,

REALLY

BRAVE!

But during the night,
when there's no light,
Dave is NOT brave.
He takes fright.

Each noise
he hears
increases
his fears.

Every
BUMP,

every
THUMP

makes his
poor heart
JUMP!

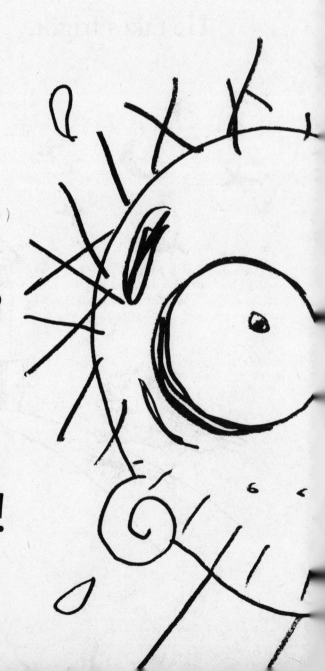

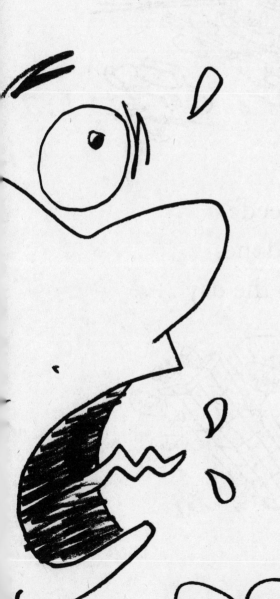

He sucks
his thumb.

He
calls
for
his
mum.

He can't wait
for the
morning
to come.

So, if you need
a brave job done,
call Dave in the day . . .

but at night,
call his mum.

RUTH'S SUPER SCOOTER

Here comes Ruth.
Ruth rides a scooter.
Ruth rides a scooter
with a super-loud hooter.

With a super-hoot here . . .

and a super-hoot there.

Here a hoot.

There a hoot.

Everywhere
a super-hoot!

We think Ruth
would be a LOT cuter
if she'd only stop blowing
her super-loud hooter.

MIKE'S BIKE

Here comes Mike.
Mike rides a bike.

Mike rides a bike
with a . . .

ve

ry

big

spike!

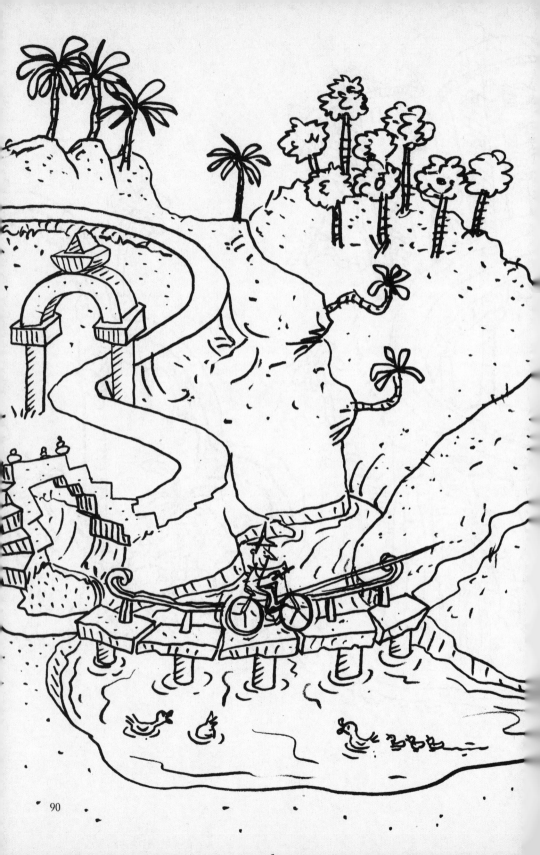

We don't like Mike
or his big, spiky bike.

Let's go somewhere
a little less Mikey!

Let's go somewhere
a little less spiky!

SOMEWHERE LESS SPIKY

Here is a town
that is really incredible.
You can eat what you like
because
everything is edible.

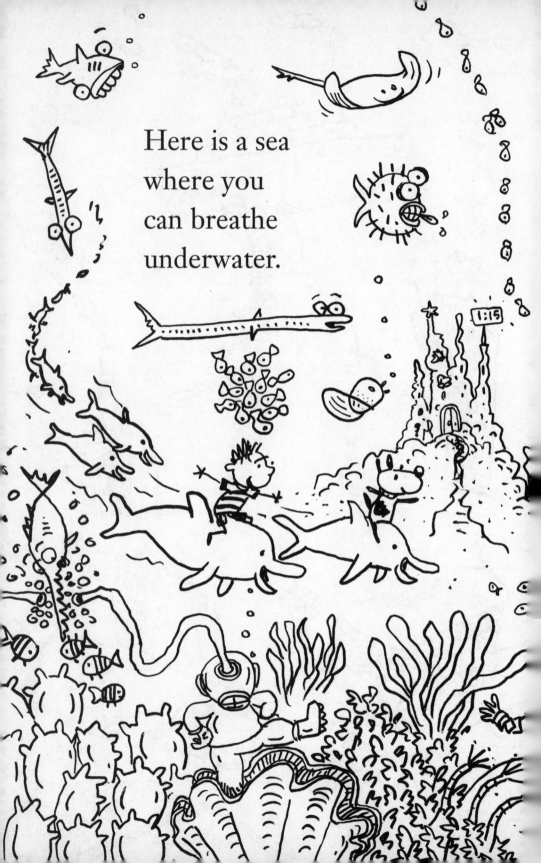

Here is a sea
where you
can breathe
underwater.

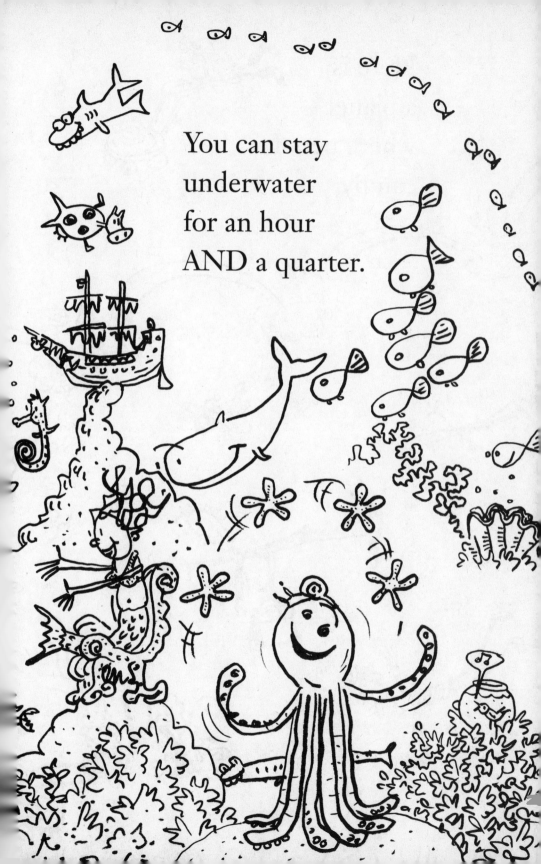

You can stay
underwater
for an hour
AND a quarter.

Here is
a planet
where people
can fly.

And the clouds
are like
trampolines
up in the sky.

103

And here is a land
with big fat
rain.

It's raining
big fat cows
again!

A big cow here.

A fat cow there.

Big fat cows are

EVERY

WHERE!

Oh, no—watch out!
Don't look now!
Here comes that
EXPLODING cow. . . .

FOUR

THREE

Go Fish!

GOFISH

ANDY GRIFFITHS

What did you want to be when you grew up?
A rock and roll singer.

When did you realize you wanted to be a writer?
When I realized I couldn't sing.

What's your first childhood memory?
Being chased around the bath by brown blobs.

What's your most embarrassing childhood memory?
Being chased around the bath by brown blobs.

What's your favorite childhood memory?
NOT being chased around the bath by brown blobs.

As a young person, who did you look up to most?
Wile E. Coyote from the Road Runner cartoon. He never gave up.

What was your worst subject in school?
Math. If only two plus two equaled five, I would have been a genius.

What was your best subject in school?
English. What's so hard about spelling hipppapotamuss?

What was your first job?
Cleaning up my bedroom. I got fired after my first day.

How did you celebrate publishing your first book?
I got a tattoo: one of the fish from Dr. Seuss's *One Fish Two Fish Red Fish Blue Fish*.

Where do you write your books?
Wherever I am . . . usually in an exercise book.

Where do you find inspiration for your writing?
In dangerous and/or embarrassing situations.

Which of your characters is most like you?
Andy Griffiths from the Just! series. It's largely autobiographical.

When you finish a book, who reads it first?
My wife, Jill.

Are you a morning person or a night owl?
I love getting up at 6:00 AM and going for a long run.

What's your idea of the best meal ever?
Pancakes with strawberries and cream.

Which do you like better: cats or dogs?
Dogs, of course. Cats are dumb. (Except for the smart ones.)

What do you value most in your friends?
That they laugh at my jokes. Even if they're not funny.

Where do you go for peace and quiet?
I close my eyes and concentrate on my breathing.

What makes you laugh out loud?
Great comedy.

What's your favorite song?
Happy Birthday to you/You live in the zoo/You look like a monkey/And you smell like one, too.

Who is your favorite fictional character?
Pinky Ponky, the shonky wonky bonky donkey.

What are you most afraid of?
Being chased around the bath by brown blobs.

What time of year do you like best?
Winter: It's much cozier to stay inside and write than in summer.

What's your favorite TV show?
Hannah Montana!

If you were stranded on a desert island, who would you want for company?
My wife.

If you could travel in time, where would you go?
Back to prehistoric times to see dinosaurs fighting. That would be cool.

What's the best advice you have ever received about writing?
Write as fast as you can without stopping or thinking about what you're writing. You can edit it later.

What do you want readers to remember about your books?
That they had a great time!

What would you do if you ever stopped writing?
Start again.

What is your worst habit?
Laughing at my own jokes.

What do you consider to be your greatest accomplishment?
Getting other people to laugh at my jokes.

Where in the world do you feel most at home?
Wherever I happen to be. But especially at home. Duh!

What do you wish you could do better?

Fix things when they're broken.

What would your readers be most surprised to learn about you?

That I'm three billion years old. It's not true, but I think my readers would be quite surprised to learn about it if it was.

GOFISH

TERRY DENTON

What did you want to be when you grew up?
I guess I always dreamed of being an artist, but never really thought it would happen. I wanted to be an animator, as well. And a zookeeper.

When did you realize you wanted to be an artist?
When I really got serious about it was when I was about twenty-two at university. I was doing cartoons in the newspaper and thought "Wow! I can do this!"

What's your first childhood memory?
Coming with my mum to the new house we had just bought and looking through the big iron gates.

What's your most embarrassing childhood memory?
Wetting my pants at school in prep class.

What's your favorite childhood memory?
Waking up one Christmas morning and my cousin had bought us a blow-up swimming pool, and it was all set up with water in the back garden. I looked down on it from my bedroom and thought I was in heaven. [Christmas in Australia is in summer.]

As a young person, who did you look up to most?
Maybe my brothers. But my childhood was remarkably free of heroes.

What was your worst subject in school?
Singing! Definitely. Still is. Also physics in secondary school.

What was your best subject in school?

We didn't have art at our school. But that would have been. Other than that, chemistry and science, in general [except physics].

What was your first job?

Working at my dad's pharmacy. Counting out pills and doing deliveries.

How did you celebrate publishing your first book?

With a satisfied smile, and got on with the next one. I don't get that big a kick out of the publication. The bit I love is when I take the finished drawings to the publisher. We often have champagne. Then it takes another six months before the book is published. By then, I am on to something else.

Where do you find inspiration for your art?

Most inspiration comes from the world and people around me. Just observing the little things.

Are you a morning person or a night owl?

Bit of a night owl. But when I had young kids, I became a morning person. But the nighttime inspires me. Gets me thinking.

What's your idea of the best meal ever?

Lobster on holidays with my family when I was young.

Which do you like better: cats or dogs?

I like cats. They are so self-contained. Dogs annoy me. They are idiots. And they eat their own sick!

What do you value most in your friends?

Friendship is the great thing about humans. I just love spending time with friends doing nothing much. Just time spent.

Where do you go for peace and quiet?

I walk to the beach, which is close by. Or my block of land about five minutes away. Or a friend's farm where we go horse-riding.

What makes you laugh out loud?

Dogs eating their own sick. Stuff my kids say. About a hundred things a day.

What's your favorite song?

"Moon River" sung by Audrey Hepburn from *Breakfast at Tiffany's.*

Who is your favorite fictional character?

Philip Marlowe from the Raymond Chandler books.

What are you most afraid of?

Death. Only because I hate leaving with the story unfinished.

What time of year do you like best?

Summer in the sun and surf, by the beach, and down in the country.

What's your favorite TV show?

The West Wing, Cowboy Bebop, and *Father Ted.*

If you were stranded on a desert island, who would you want for company?

My friend Tim, but don't tell my wife. Tim and I would have fun making a boat and fishing and turn it into a Swiss Family Robinson event.

If you could travel in time, where would you go?

Maybe to 2070 to see what kind of world we have by then. And to see my kids grown up.

What's the best advice you have ever received about drawing?

Draw what you love drawing. And follow your instincts.

What would you do if you ever stopped drawing?

Decompose.

What do you like best about yourself?

That I care for people and that I <u>do</u> trust my instincts.

What is your worst habit?

Trying to do too much instead of having a bit of space in my day so I can think.

What do you consider to be your greatest accomplishment?

I guess when I see my kids; I think that is hard to beat.

Where in the world do you feel most at home?
At home. Where my family is. And there is a place 200 kilometers away from where I live that I often go to. A national park called Wilsons Promontory. And I feel very close to that.

What do you wish you could do better?
Sing!!!!!!!!!!

What would readers be most surprised to learn about you?
There is nothing surprising about me.

Get ready for another laugh attack!

The Cat on the Mat Is Flat

Written by Andy Griffiths; Illustrated by Terry Denton

978-0-312-53584-1 · $6.99 US / $8.99 Can.

Muck! Uck! Yuck!

It's just bad luck

when the truck of a duck

gets stuck in the muck.

Or when a dog on a cog

gets chased by a frog

**around the bog of
an angry hog.**

All of this and so much more!

**We promise it won't
be a snore!**

**These wacky rhymes just
don't bore!**

SQUARE FISH
WWW.SQUAREFISHBOOKS.COM
AVAILABLE WHEREVER BOOKS ARE SOLD